DOYLE AND FOSSEY, SCIENCE DETECTIVES

The Case of the Graveyard Ghost

(and Other Super-Scientific Cases)

MICHELE TORREY

ILLUSTRATED BY
BARBARA JOHANSEN NEWMAN

STERLING CHILDREN'S BOOKS
New York

To my Grandmother June, who giggles at silly things still

Also to Heather and Judy—four cheers for soup,
coffee, laughter, and red ink

My thanks to Professor Dave Wall,
Department of Physics, City College of San Francisco,
for his help with "Pepper's Ghost."
M. T.

For my three sons, David, Mike, and Ben—you love,
you inspire, and you keep me on my toes!
B. J. N.

STERLING CHILDREN'S BOOKS
New York

An Imprint of Sterling Publishing
387 Park Avenue South
New York, NY 10016

STERLING CHILDREN'S BOOKS and the distinctive Sterling Children's Books logo are
trademarks of Sterling Publishing Co., Inc.

Text © 2002, 2009 by Michele Torrey
Illustrations © 2002, 2009 Barbara Johansen Newman

ISBN 978-1-4027-4963-6

Distributed in Canada by Sterling Publishing
C/o Canadian Manda Group, 165 Dufferin Street
Toronto, Ontario, Canada M6K 3H6
Distributed in the United Kingdom by GMC Distribution Services
Castle Place, 166 High Street, Lewes, East Sussex, England BN7 1XU
Distributed in Australia by Capricorn Link (Australia) Pty. Ltd.
P.O. Box 704, Windsor, NSW 2756, Australia

For information about custom editions, special sales, and premium and corporate purchases,
please contact Sterling Special Sales at 800-805-5489 or specialsales@sterlingpublishing.com.

Manufactured in the United States of America

Lot #:
4 6 8 10 9 7 5 3
08/12
This book originally published in hardcover by Dutton Children's Books in 2002.

www.sterlingpublishing.com/kids

CONTENTS

CHAPTER ONE

A Noisy Cupboard

From the sidewalk, the attic looked like any other attic. It had cute little windows with yellow curtains and a soft light glowing from behind. But everyone in the small town of Mossy Lake knew this was no ordinary attic. No, indeed.

It was a laboratory.

A top-notch laboratory at that.

Inside was top-notch equipment, and a top-notch scientist as well. His name was Drake Doyle. He looked quite scientific with his lab coat and his glasses that always slid to the end of his nose. And if that wasn't enough, his cinnamon-colored hair looked as if it had actually exploded once, or twice, or perhaps three times. (In fact, Drake's hair looked rather like a science experiment itself.)

On this fine Saturday, Drake squeezed a drop of liquid into a swirling solution.

"Aha!" he declared as the bright pink solution suddenly turned clear.

He scribbled in his lab notebook.

One more drop.
Solution neutralized.
Analysis complete.

But before he could even slap his notebook shut, the phone rang. "Doyle and Fossey," he answered, removing his safety goggles and shoving his pencil behind his ear.

Now, in case you didn't know, Nell Fossey was Drake's science and business partner. (And his best friend.) They did most everything together, especially when it came to solving their many cases. Their business cards read:

Doyle and Fossey:
Science Detectives
call us. anytime. 555-7822

They were a good team. A fabulous team. A top-notch team. The best scientific team in the entire fifth grade.

"I demand to speak with Drake Doyle at once," snapped the caller, whose voice sounded strangely muffled.

"Speaking," replied Drake.

"Well, it's about time. I don't have all day, you know."

Drake blinked with surprise. The caller was quite rude. But, no matter. For besides being an amateur scientist and detective genius, Drake Doyle was a professional. And professionals never lose their cool. Even if their clients are rude. Quite rude. "And who, may I ask, is calling?" Drake inquired, in his most polite and professional voice.

"It's Sloane Westcott. Who else, beaker brain?"

Drake should have known it was Sloane. Everyone agreed that if there was an award for rudeness, Sloane Westcott would be the winner. Hands down. She was the most impolite student in the fifth grade. She never said "please," and she most certainly never said "thank you," or "nice day, isn't it?" But, business was business, and a professional must be a professional. So Drake asked, "What seems to be the problem, Ms. Westcott?"

"Listen, you little lab rat, let me make one thing perfectly clear. Frisco was my first choice—"

"Hmm. I see," said Drake.

Now, as luck would have it, James Frisco was in Drake and Nell's class at school. Like them, he was a scientist. But he was a bad scientist. Actually, a *mad* scientist. While Drake always followed instructions, Frisco tore up instructions, or lost them, or accidentally-on-purpose set them on fire. While Drake measured carefully, Frisco didn't even own a measuring cup, or a measuring spoon, and often closed his eyes while pouring something out of a bottle.

Frisco's business cards read:

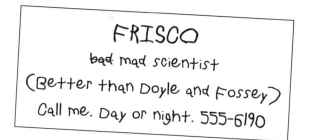

FRISCO
~~bad~~ mad scientist
(Better than Doyle and Fossey)
Call me. Day or night. 555-6190

Now, normally when someone threatened to hire Frisco, Drake did everything he could to talk them out of such foolishness. But, on this particular day, with this particular client, Drake merely said, "Hmm. I see," while trying to sound terribly disappointed. "Very well, then, it's been a pleasure talking with you—"

"Wait! Don't hang up! Uh—what I mean is,

Frisco's out of town and, well—uh, I have a slight situation. . . ."

After listening for a minute or two, Drake politely said good-bye and hung up, resisting the urge to laugh. (Laughing at customers is definitely unscientific.) Instead he called Nell. "Scientist Nell, meet me at Sloane Westcott's house. Five minutes and counting. Sloane's in a tight spot and requires our assistance immediately."

"Check."

Click.

When Drake arrived at Sloane's house, Nell was already waiting by the front door. (She was the fastest runner in the fifth grade, so Drake was used to being the last to arrive. Not to mention that he tripped once on his way over . . . well, maybe twice.) With her coffee-colored hair in a ponytail, and a pencil behind each ear, Nell looked ready for business. Important business. "Doesn't look like anyone's home," observed Nell as she peered through the keyhole. "The house is dark and the curtains are drawn."

"Trust me," replied Drake, and he opened the front door and walked in.

"Are you sure this is okay?" asked Nell. "To just walk in without knocking?"

Drake flicked on his flashlight and pushed up his glasses. "Trust me," he said again. And up the stairs he went. (He tripped only once.)

In the second bedroom on the right, he found what he was looking for. "Aha!"

"What?"

"Observe, Scientist Nell." And he aimed his flashlight at a cupboard in the wall.

Now, Nell was a sharp scientist. A genius scientist, to be more accurate. She noticed immediately that this cupboard was not like most cupboards. First of all, the cupboard doors lay flat against the wall, like a medicine cabinet. Second, the cupboard was making strange noises. That's right. It was a noisy cupboard. Squeals and yelps could be faintly heard from inside. *Inside the wall*, to be precise. "Hmm," she mused.

While Nell stood there musing, Drake went to work. He pushed up his sleeves. He adjusted his glasses. He cleared his throat. He waved his flashlight around. He opened the little doors.

And together they peered into the cupboard.

CHAPTER TWO
Blast Off!

Actually, they didn't peer *into* the cupboard.

They peered *down* the cupboard. Because it was not really a cupboard at all. It was a laundry chute. The chute went all the way from the bedroom to the laundry room, two stories below.

Down, down, down it went. And halfway down, they saw something strange.

It was a pair of tennis shoes. Perhaps a pair of tennis shoes wouldn't be too strange a thing to find in a laundry chute, except that attached to these tennis shoes was a pair of *legs*.

"Sloane?" Drake hollered down the chute, his voice echoing. "Sloane? Is that you?"

"Who else would it be?" a voice screeched. "The mayor? Or maybe the president of the United

8

States? Yeah. That's right. The president. I'm going to give a speech to my dirty underwear."

Drake closed the cupboard doors and looked at Nell. "It's her, all right."

"How did she call you if she's stuck in the laundry chute?" asked Nell.

"That's just it," explained Drake. "She was cleaning her room and accidentally threw her cell phone down the chute along with some dirty clothes. When she lunged after the phone, she fell in. The good news is, she caught her cell phone. The bad news is, she's been stuck upside down ever since her mom went to work this afternoon."

"Why didn't Sloane call 911?"

"She told me she'd be grounded and lose her allowance," answered Drake. (He decided not to mention that Sloane had also told him to stop asking her so many questions, and that she had called him a pencil-pocket, geek-breath scientist with a brain no bigger than an atom.)

"So, what's the plan?" asked Nell.

Drake scratched his head, baffled. "We must return to the lab for analysis."

"Check."

Wanting to avoid further insults, they hurried to the lab before giving Sloane a quick phone call to tell her they had left. "Uh, you call her," said Drake, handing the phone to Nell.

She dialed the number. As soon as Sloane answered, Nell said as fast as she could, "We'll-be-back-in-half-an-hour-bye," and hung up. "Okay," she said to Drake, "down to business."

Drake pulled a book off the shelf. Together they thumbed through to find the right section: "Laundry Chute Extraction: What to Do When Someone Is Stuck, and They're Being Quite Rude." Nell read the section aloud, and Drake took notes.

A little later, Drake's mom opened the attic door and peeked in. "Hot chocolate, anyone? Juice? Muffins?" Whenever Kate Doyle offered muffins, it was best to say yes, because her muffins were delicious. In fact, Mrs. Doyle owned a catering company and was a fine person to have nearby, especially if you became hungry or thirsty.

"Muffins, if you please," said Drake politely.

"Affirmative," replied Mrs. Doyle.

"Coffee," said Nell. "Decaf. Black." (Real scientists don't drink hot chocolate. They prefer coffee. Decaf. Black.)

"Check," said Mrs. Doyle, returning just fifteen and a half seconds later with their order. (She must have known they were in the middle of a laundry-chute-extraction emergency, and had the muffins and coffee standing by, ready to go.)

Nell took a sip of coffee and then phoned her mother. "Won't be home until later," Nell told her. "Much later. Laundry-chute-extraction emergency, you know."

Nell wasn't a bit surprised when Professor Fossey replied, "I understand, my dear. Do what you think is best."

You see, Nell was a lucky scientist because her mother was also a scientist. Ann Fossey taught wildlife biology at Mossy Lake University. So she understood perfectly about scientific emergencies and not being home until later.

Twenty minutes after that, Drake and Nell stood outside on the sidewalk, ready. Their bikes were loaded with the necessary supplies.

Just then, Drake's dad, Sam Doyle, drove into the driveway. Like Mrs. Doyle, Mr. Doyle was pretty handy to have around. He was great for giving rides and good conversation. Not only that, but he owned his own company, too: Doyle's Science Equipment and Supply Company. He provided everything Drake and Nell needed for a well-equipped lab: pencils, test tubes, computers, glassware, and, of course, lab coats with their names on them. "Going somewhere?" asked Mr. Doyle.

"We're on a case," said Drake and Nell together.

"Need a ride?"

"Thanks just the same, Mr. Doyle, but we've got it covered," Nell replied.

Then Mr. Doyle took a long look at the items on their bikes and said, "Whatever you do, don't blow up anything."

Drake and Nell looked at each other, because, you see, *that's exactly what they planned to do!* (All in the name of science, of course.)

"Thanks for the advice, Mr. Doyle," said Nell quickly, "but our client is waiting."

"Bye, Dad!" called Drake over his shoulder. And off they went, riding like the wind.

When they arrived at Sloane's house, they immediately got to work.

Drake lugged all the supplies upstairs to Sloane's room while Nell went down the dusty basement steps to prepare the laundry room. Nell gathered the dirty clothes into a huge pile. She added a bunch of pillows and sofa cushions just to be on the safe side.

Meanwhile, Sloane's voice blasted through

the laundry chute. "What's going on out there? I demand you tell me! If you don't get me out of here in two seconds, I'm calling my lawyer!" Pause . . . "Okay, that's it! I've had it with you people! I'm dialing!"

BEEP! beep! boop! boop! bop! beep! BUP!

"Did you hear that?" Sloane screeched. "Huh? Did you hear that? I dialed! And it's ringing!"

Their preparations completed, Drake and Nell stood together next to the laundry chute in Sloane's room. "Ready?" Drake asked.

Nell nodded. "All set in the laundry room. The pile is eight feet high, with a diameter of twelve feet."

"Good work, Scientist Nell. Let us begin."

"Agreed, Detective Doyle. Before she sues our socks off."

"Check," replied Drake. First, he poured five boxes of baking soda he'd found in his mom's kitchen pantry down the laundry chute.

"Hey!" screamed Sloane. "I felt that!"

Drake hollered down the chute. "Ahoy down there! Squeezing your eyes shut is highly recommended!"

And while Sloane told Drake what he could do with his high recommendations, Drake held a large bucket full of vinegar over the opening. "As soon as I finish pouring it in," he said to Nell, "you slam the cupboard doors shut."

"Roger that."

Drake poured the vinegar down the chute.

"Hey!" shrieked Sloane. "You're getting me all wet!"

"Now!" cried Drake.

"Check!" exclaimed Nell.

Slam!

Then they raced down two flights of stairs to the laundry room. And then, from inside the chute came a moan . . .

"Just try to relax, Ms. Westcott!" cried Drake. "This won't hurt a bit!"

. . . and a groan . . .

"Prepare for blastoff!" he hollered. "Ten, nine, eight—"

. . . and a mumble . . .

"Seven, six—"

. . . and a rumble . . .

"Five, four—"

. . . plus a grumble . . .

"Three, two, one—"

Then the house heaved like a hiccup!

"Blast off!" screamed Nell.

. . . suddenly, in an explosion of bubbles and fizz, out flew Sloane!

Whoosh! Fizzle!

"AAAaaaaa!"

Zoom! Plop! Splat! Sloane landed headfirst in the enormous pile of clothes. Dirty laundry flew everywhere.

"Incredible!" exclaimed Drake.

"Remarkable!" cried Nell.

It was quite spectacular, really. Better than the Fourth of July. Both Drake and Nell enjoyed it thoroughly.

When Sloane could finally speak, she moaned, "Ohhhhh. Am I alive?"

"Quite so," replied Drake.

"What—what day is it? Who am I? Where are we? What happened? What's two plus two?"

"Allow my partner to explain," said Drake, tossing Sloane a clean towel. "Ms. Fossey?"

Nell cleared her throat and paced the laundry room. "After we observed that you were stuck in the laundry chute, we knew we needed something to blast you out of there."

"Quite so," added Drake.

"By adding baking soda—" continued Nell.

"—and vinegar—" said Drake.

"—we caused a strong chemical reaction. We no longer had baking soda and vinegar—"

"Indeed no," added Drake.

"Instead we created an entirely new substance." Nell stopped pacing and looked quite serious, as good scientists often do. "The baking soda and vinegar reacted to form carbon-dioxide gas. The pressure of the gas was so great—"

"—that it blew you completely out of the laundry chute," finished Drake.

"Oooh," moaned Sloane, holding her head. "Thanks . . . I think."

Nell climbed the mountain of laundry. She handed her business card to Sloane. "Take a shower. Then go straight to bed. Call us first thing in the morning."

That evening, back at the lab, Drake wrote in his lab notebook:

Laundry chute extraction complete.
Sloane friendly for first time.
(A scientific phenomenon to be studied further.)
Received one month of free cellular phone service.
        Paid in full.

17

CHAPTER THREE

An Irregular Situation

It was a gray, gloomy, damp Saturday morning, the perfect sort of weather for testing the sogginess of breakfast cereals. Drake took a bite of sample #27. He chewed this way and that way, and then swallowed just so.

"Hmm," he mused. Taking a pencil out from behind his ear, he recorded his conclusions in his lab notebook.

> SAMPLE #27: Not terribly soggy, but certainly not highly crunchy.
> SF = 4

(In scientific circles, the sog measuring scale is known as the Sog Factor (SF), where 1=terribly soggy and 10=highly crunchy.)

After rinsing out his mouth with water, Drake took a bite of sample #28.

Just then, the phone rang.

"Doyle and Fossey," he answered. (Actually, it sounded more like "Dooyyye-nnn-Fffffofffyy.")

"Detective Doyle," said the caller in a trembly voice, "I daresay I have a highly irregular situation."

Drake spat his cereal into the sink. SF determinations would have to wait. After all, this was a highly irregular situation. "Who's calling?"

"It's Mary. Mary Elizabeth Pendleton." Mary was in Drake and Nell's class at school. Mary was, very simply, a proper young lady. She never slouched in her chair or yelled at recess. She always wore dresses and used her lace handkerchief whenever she sneezed. Lastly, but most enjoyably, she threw charming garden parties where she served tea and crumpets while saying such witty things as "If you would be so kind" and "Jolly good weather, isn't it?" and "More tea?" while every now and then reciting a lovely poem.

Mary was the exact opposite of rude Sloane Westcott, and Drake felt more than a little relieved. (After all, there is a limit to the number of insults a top-notch scientist can bear.) "What can I do for you, Ms. Pendleton?" Drake asked.

"I'm here at the Budding Botanists Junior Rose Club. It would be ever so splendid if you could hurry over. Of course, I'll explain everything when you arrive."

"Ten minutes and counting. You have my word."

"Cheerio, ol' chap," she replied, and hung up.

Drake called Nell. "Highly irregular situation at the Budding Botanists Junior Rose Club," he told her. "Nine minutes fifty-three seconds, and counting."

"Check."

Click.

Fortunately, Drake felt quite fortified after eating so much cereal. He pedaled his bike like fury, slowing down only once when he fell—*crash! sploosh!*—into a muddy pothole. (He was wearing his helmet and rain gear, and wasn't hurt a bit.)

"Ready, Detective Doyle?" Nell asked, once he'd screeched to a stop at the Junior Rose Club.

"Ready, Scientist Nell," he replied.

Nell helped him lock up his bike. Together they entered the double doors, dripping as they went.

"So kind of you to come," said Mary, shaking their hands daintily.

"What seems to be the trouble, Ms. Pendleton?" asked Nell as they hung up their raincoats.

Mary dabbed her eyes with a hankie. "Perhaps it would be easier if you'd just come with me. As they say, a picture is worth a thousand words."

Drake glanced at Nell. He removed his detective kit and notebook from his backpack and shoved a pencil behind his ear. (A scientist is always prepared. Even in the gloomiest of weather. Even in the most irregular of situations.) "Lead the way, Ms. Pendleton."

They followed Mary into a large room where a few dozen club members milled about. A banner overhead read: ANNUAL BUDDING BOTANISTS JUNIOR ROSE CLUB COMPETITION! PRIZES GALORE! Bouquets of roses were displayed on tables.

They smelled . . . absolutely heavenly.

They looked . . . absolutely disgusting.

"Great Scott!" cried Drake.

"This is dreadful!" cried Nell.

"Yes." Mary nodded, wiping away a tear. "Perfectly dreadful. See this bouquet?" She pointed at a bouquet on the table beside her. The label read:

EXHIBIT #19
SPECIES: ANGEL GLORY

"This is my entry. Yesterday the blossoms were a stunning, pure white. Today, well"—gasp!— "they're the color of . . . the color of . . . dare I say . . . *swamp slime!*"

And indeed, she was right.

All around the room, the roses were the nastiest of colors—mold, barf, dirt, snot, slug, grasshopper gut—if such colors really could be called colors at all.

Drake flipped open his lab notebook. "When was this first discovered?" he asked.

"At eight o'clock this morning, when everyone arrived to set up for the show," replied Mary. "Yesterday we cut our bouquets in the greenhouse and stored them overnight in the walk-in refrigerator. When we went to fetch them this morning, well, naturally, we were all stunned. I imagine the judge will have a most difficult time of it."

"When is the judging?" asked Nell.

Mary glanced at her watch. "Dearie me. In just an hour and a half."

"Hey, Mary!" someone hollered from behind them.

It was Tess O'Brien, another classmate. Tess was an earthy sort of person—at one with the universe, aligned with the planets, and all that.

She always wore shorts and sandals, even when the weather was gloomy. Today her fingernails were a mite crusty around the edges, and she smelled a little like not-so-fresh air. "Peace be with you," she sighed, giving Mary a down-to-earth hug. "Sorry your roses look like swamp slime."

"Thank you, Tess, why, thank you indeed," Mary replied, stepping back and smoothing her dress. "Sorry about your roses, as well."

Tess sighed again. "Must've been the water."

"That's what we're here to find out," said Drake. "Have you noticed anything unusual?"

Tess shook her head. "Nothing. I was the first one here because I always wake up with the sunrise. Of course, the roses were already ruined. I called Mary right away. Like I said. Must've been the water."

After questioning Tess and Mary, Drake and Nell set to work. They pulled on surgical gloves. *Snap!*

They took out magnifying glasses. They examined the roses. They jotted notes. Drew charts. Took water samples. Pushed buttons on their calculators. Then, just as they completed a search of the premises, their archenemy appeared.

That's right. Frisco walked through the door.

CHAPTER FOUR

A Dirty Deed

"**E**gads!" exclaimed Drake, his glasses slipping down his nose. "What's *he* doing here?"

"Someone else must have hired him," said Mary. "After all, we're not the only ones from our class who are in the Budding Botanists Junior Rose Club. There's Peter Underwood, who won last year, and, of course, Sloane Westcott. Her mother makes her."

And as they watched, horrified, Frisco declared to all, "I'm here to save the day."

Everyone gathered around him, clapping and exclaiming.

Peter Underwood approached Frisco, and while neither Drake nor Nell could hear what they said, they shook hands while Frisco handed him a business card. Behind them, Sloane Westcott stamped her foot and said, "What about me?" So he handed her a business card as well.

Then Frisco whipped out his magnifying glass and began examining a bouquet of slime-colored roses.

"Quick, Scientist Nell," exclaimed Drake, pushing up his glasses. "We have no time to lose! We must find the solution before Frisco saves the day!"

"Check!"

Without wasting another second, they threw on their rain gear and hustled out the door.

"To the lab!" cried Drake as he climbed on his bike.

"For further analysis!" cried Nell as she climbed on hers.

"Peace, my people," said Tess, giving the peace sign.

"Oh, do be careful," cried Mary as she waved good-bye with her white hankie.

The lab was quite comfy, just the thing after pedaling through mud puddles and gloom. Once inside, Drake pulled a book off the shelf and joined Nell at the lab table. Together they found the right section: "Irregular Situations: What to Do When Your Roses Look Like Swamp Slime and Your Archenemy Vows to Save the Day."

After they read the section, they shared their observations. They jotted. They sharpened pencils. They scratched their heads. They thought very hard. And through all this head-scratching and hard-thinking, they developed a hypothesis. (All good scientists know that a hypothesis is merely their best guess as to what is happening.)

"We must test our hypothesis," said Nell firmly.

"Check," said Drake.

And so they did. (With a little help from Mrs. Doyle.)

Afterward, Nell said with a satisfied nod, "Just as we thought."

"Indeed," replied Drake. "Our hypothesis is correct."

They gathered their evidence and hurried back to the Budding Botanists Junior Rose Club, arriving just in the nick of time. All the club members were seated at the front of the room facing Frisco.

"And finally," Frisco was saying, "my scientific conclusion is, it was the water. Without a doubt, it was definitely the water. I'm sure of it. Positive. No other possible explanation." And he sat down with a smirk. Peter Underwood shook Frisco's hand and thanked him for getting to the bottom of the matter. In return, Frisco handed Peter a bill.

"Oh, dear me," said the judge, rising from his seat. He shuffled through some papers on his clipboard. "Ahem. Well then, I hate to be the bearer of bad news, but seeing as the water was bad, this year's contest is . . . um . . . *cancel—*"

"Hold everything!" cried Drake and Nell. Everyone gasped as they stepped to the front of the room. Drake unzipped his backpack and withdrew a bouquet of roses. They were a stunning pale pink. The color of a morning sunrise. Quite lovely, indeed.

"Ooh," breathed the audience.

Then Drake withdrew another bouquet of roses from his backpack. This bouquet, however, was not so lovely. In fact, it was downright ugly. It was . . . the color of . . . bird doo.

The audience gasped in horror. *"Eeww!"*

"Just this morning," said Drake in his most professional voice, "these were all beautiful roses."

"Mrs. Doyle's roses," added Nell, "which she generously donated."

28

"All in the name of science," remarked Drake as he began to pace the room. "Earlier, we conducted a thorough examination of the competition roses. Based upon our observations, we suspected something was not right. Not right at all. Allow Scientist Nell to explain."

"Thank you, Detective Doyle. First of all, we noticed some discoloration along the rose stems. Second, at the site of each discoloration was a tiny hole, as if the stems had been pricked by a pin."

"Most suspicious," Drake commented, stopping his pacing. He raised his eyebrow at the audience.

"Indeed," agreed Nell. "We developed a hypothesis and tested it. Worked like a charm. You see the results before you. Bird-doo-doo roses."

"Yes—quite," said Mary. "But how *did* you do it?"

"Excellent question, Ms. Pendleton," Drake responded. "We're coming to that."

"Hopefully after I leave," griped Frisco.

Nell clasped her hands behind her and began to pace. "Ask yourselves this question: If a tree doesn't have a heart to pump liquid through its system, then how does water travel from its roots all the way to the top of the tree?"

"The answer is, of course, capillary action," Drake replied. "Instead of veins, plants have capillaries—"

"—which are very tiny tubes," added Nell.

"You see, water molecules are rather sticky," said Drake.

"If you spill water on a table," Nell continued, "water molecules stick together in a puddle. In the same way, water molecules climb up the sides of a capillary tube, sticking together and traveling through the plant. It's quite remarkable, really."

"And your point is—?" said Peter Underwood, frowning.

Drake replied calmly, "The perpetrator simply injected dye into the stems, using a hypodermic syringe. Capillary action transported the dye through the roses, changing their blossoms into different colors."

"But why?" asked Mary. "Why would anyone do something so dreadfully rotten?"

And then there followed a great silence, because, after all, it really was an excellent question. And no one had an excellent answer.

Except one.

Suddenly, Tess O'Brien crumpled to the floor.

"I confess! I confess! It was me! I did it! I did the dirty deed!" She put her face in her hands and sobbed. Oh, sobbed quite terribly.

Everyone gasped, including Drake and Nell.

"But why?" Mary asked again.

For a moment, Tess didn't answer because she was so busy sobbing. But finally she wiped her eyes and blew her nose on her sleeve. "Because I'm so *horrible* at gardening. Because every year someone *else* wins. Because . . . because . . . well, just *look* at my bouquet! It's not only slimy, it's *puny*! I mean, after all, I'm supposed to be *earthy*. People who are earthy should be whizzes at gardening! I couldn't stand it anymore! I cracked under the pressure!"

"There, there," murmured Mary, and she put her arm around Tess.

It was quite a hubbub.

In the end, Mary agreed to help Tess by giving her private gardening lessons. In return, Tess would help Mary align her planets. All in all, everyone was quite satisfied.

"Call us, anytime," said Drake, handing Mary his business card.

"I shall, I shall," said Mary. "You and Nell have proved ever so brilliant. Cheerio!"

Later that day, Drake wrote in his lab notebook:

Swamp-Slime Rose case solved.
Tess used Super-Soupy
Swampy Slime Juice & Other
Disgusting Dyes, developed
and sold by Frisco.
Received open invitation to all
future garden parties.
   Paid in Full.
   _____

CHAPTER FIVE

A Blustery Night

It was a blustery night, perfect for charting the growth of guppies. So, after washing the dishes and feeding her animals, Nell sat at her desk and flipped on the lamp. Ten seconds later, the phone rang.

"Doyle and Fossey," she answered, shoving her pencil behind her ear.

It was Drake. "Have you read today's copy of *The Frisco Files*?"

"Negative."

"Read the cover story. There's no time to lose."

"Check." Nell set down the receiver and dug in her school backpack. Every week, Frisco published and sold his own science newsletter for five cents per copy. Although a nickel was too much money for such bad science, Drake and Nell always wanted to know what Frisco was up to.

Nell read, her eyes growing larger by the second.

Graveyard Ghost FOR REAL!!!
(Not Fake!)

Last night at the Old Mossy Graveyard, several witnesses watched as Sloane Westcott conjured up a real ghost. The ghost made horrible sounds, including, but not limited to, clanking its chains and moaning. Plus it had lots of blood. Sloane will conjure up the ghost again tonight (Friday) at 8:00 P.M. All are invited. Only $1.00 each.

"This is bad," said Nell, shaking her head.

"Agreed," replied Drake.

"And did you notice that today at school we could hardly give away copies of our own newsletter?" asked Nell. Drake and Nell also published a weekly newsletter called *Amazing Science for Geniuses and the Merely Curious*. This week their newsletter detailed Sloane Westcott's laundry-chute blastoff. (Needless to say, Sloane was *not* amused.)

"We gave away only five copies," said Drake, "as opposed to our usual ninety."

"While Frisco's newsletter was selling like hotcakes," said Nell.

"Here's the deal," Drake said, sounding very serious. "Our reputation is at stake. Therefore, we must go to the graveyard to investigate. Dad and I will pick you up at seven-fifty sharp."

"Check."

Click.

Old Mossy Graveyard was the oldest, spookiest graveyard in town. Not only did it have crumbling, lichen-covered tombstones, but it also had twisted trees and things that went *bump!* and *oooh!* in the night.

Fortunately, tonight was a full moon. Perfect for investigating. And as Drake, Nell, and Dr. Livingston, Nell's dog, clambered out of the car, the wind moaned, sounding perfectly haunted.

"Don't be long," said Mr. Doyle. And, like all the other parents in all the other cars, he turned on the interior light, rolled down his window, and opened his newspaper. "Scream if you need me."

"Roger that," said Drake and Nell as they shut the car door.

Up the winding path near the gardener's shed, they saw a line of kids. Sloane was taking their money. "That'll be one dollar. Seat 3C. Next!"

When Sloane saw Drake and Nell, she frowned. "Wouldn't you know. It's the beaker-brain twins and their dumb dog."

Nell ignored Sloane and whipped out three dollars. "My treat," Nell said to Drake and Dr. Livingston.

"Seats 4A, B, and C," snapped Sloane. "They're the crummiest seats I've got. And no funny detective stuff, or I'll kick you out. And no refunds."

Once Nell took her seat, with Drake on one side and Dr. Livingston on the other, the show began.

Sloane stood before the audience. "Welcome to the greatest ghost show on earth! And without further ado, let's begin." She waved her arms around, sprinkled some glittery dust, and said, "Abracadabra! Presto chango! Hocus pocus! Alakazam!"

Nothing.

More glittery dust. "Abracadabra! Presto chango! Hocus pocus! Alakazam!"

Nothing.

"Ahem. Maybe you didn't hear me. I *said*, Abracadabra! Presto chango! Hocus pocus! And Alaka-ZAM! ARE YOU DEAF, OR WHAT?!"

And then, just as Nell was about to cross her arms smugly, there appeared . . .

. . . *a ghost.*

A chill swept up Nell's spine as both the ghost and the wind began to howl. Beside her, Dr. Livingston growled. Drake almost fell off his chair.

"Oh my gosh," whispered Nell. "I can't believe it. *It's real.*"

CHAPTER SIX
The Ghost of Mossy Lake

The ghost was terrifying.

Ghoulish.

Wrapped in chains and dripping with blood, it waved its arms about, moaning.

And then, as if blood and chains and moans weren't enough, Sloane walked *right through* the ghost. "I am not afraid," she declared, with her hands on her hips.

"AAAAHHHH!!!!!!" screamed the audience.

"Fascinating," murmured Drake.

"Scary," whispered Nell.

Grrr, growled Dr. Livingston.

And then the ghost began to speak. "*Ooooooh! I ammmm the ghossst of Mossssy Laaaake. Yoooou muuuusssst doooooo what I sssssaaaaay. Yoooou muuuussst*

40

put all your moneeeeeeyyyy innnn the jaaarrr, or else
I will haunt you forrrevvvver! Ooooooooooh!"

"AAAAHHHH!!!!!!" screamed the audience again.

"Hmm," murmured Drake.

"Sounds fishy," whispered Nell.

Grrr, growled Dr. Livingston.

Soon the clink of money filled the air.

Nell ignored the money jar and took notes in her notebook, using her handy-dandy flashlight pen. Every now and then, Drake whispered his observations in her ear, which she jotted down as well. But there was something about the ghost's voice that wasn't quite right. Something Nell couldn't put her finger on. It bothered her, rather like having an itch where you can't scratch. Meanwhile, Dr. Livingston disappeared.

The show was over. "Same show tomorrow night," said Sloane. "Five bucks each. Tell your friends. Now scram."

Just then, Dr. Livingston bounded up with something in his mouth. Once in the car, Nell examined it. "Hmm. It appears to be a piece of the ghost's bloody sheet."

Drake held it to his nose. "Smeared with ketchup, no less."

"Was it a trick?" asked Mr. Doyle as he drove home.

Nell nodded. "No doubt. The sheet with ketchup proves it. But how they did it is the question. It was remarkable."

"Indeed." Drake pushed up his glasses. "The case has me baffled. Let's return to the graveyard tomorrow to search for clues. That is—if it's all right with you, Dad."

"Affirmative," said Mr. Doyle.

The next evening at dusk, they found a few footprints around the grave and tombstone where Sloane had been standing. "Same shoe size and print," said Nell, disappointed. "Likely Sloane's footprints."

"Ground's solid," observed Drake, jumping up and down a few times. "The ghost couldn't have risen from the soil. No trees overhead to dangle a ghost from either."

They circled the area. They scanned the sky. They checked behind tombstones. And just as they were about to give up, they walked into something hard and flat and invisible.

"Ow!" cried Drake.

"Ow!" cried Nell.

Arf! cried Dr. Livingston.

Nell rubbed her nose. "What the—"

Drake got up and brushed himself off. (He'd fallen backward onto his behind.) "It's a large sheet of plastic glass," he said, rapping on its surface. "Propped up between tombstones. Invisible to the audience."

"Yes, but why?" Nell frowned. This case was becoming more puzzling by the minute.

But before Drake could answer, Dr. Livingston took off toward the gardener's shed.

Suddenly Nell had a hunch. She followed Dr. Livingston and tried the door. It opened.

Creeeeak!

"Follow me, Detective Doyle," she hollered as she entered the shed.

It was dark and dusty inside. Nell flicked on her pocket pen flashlight. Of course, there was the usual gardener's stuff. Shovels, rakes, hoes, and the like. But there was some other stuff that didn't belong—a white sheet smeared with ketchup, and a pile of chains. Not your normal everyday gardening stuff.

"Aha," whispered Drake.

"Hmm," murmured Nell.

Grrr, growled Dr. Livingston.

Nell lifted the sheet. "There's also a slide projector here. And a bottle of ketchup. You know, Detective Doyle, something bothered me about the ghost last night. Now I realize what it was."

"What?"

"The voice of the ghost wasn't coming from where the ghost was standing."

"Great Scott!" exclaimed Drake. "You're right! The voice of the ghost was coming from—"

"—*inside this shed*," they said together.

"And last night," continued Drake, "if I recall correctly, the door to the shed was open, although from where we were sitting, we couldn't see inside."

"Hmm." Nell thought very hard. "And straight out from the open doorway is—"

"—the sheet of plastic glass!" finished Drake.

"I think I'm beginning to get the picture," said Nell.

"Ditto," replied Drake. "Let's return to the lab for analysis."

"And then," Nell hollered over her shoulder as she flew out the door and down the path, "it's show time!"

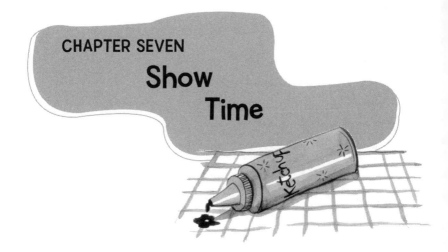

CHAPTER SEVEN

Show Time

Later that night, silvery moonlight filtered through the trees and into the graveyard. All was still and silent. A creepy fog slithered around the tombstones. An owl hooted.

Drake, Nell, and Dr. Livingston watched from the back row as Sloane waved her arms, sprinkled glitter, and chanted her magical words.

Suddenly the ghost appeared and clanked his chains. *"Ooooooooooh! I ammmm the ghossst of Mossssy Laaaake. . . ."*

But the audience, instead of screaming, instead of covering their eyes in terror, instead of digging in their pockets for all their money . . . *began to laugh.*

That's right. Laugh!

Because written with ketchup on the front of the ghost's sheet were the words: I AM A FAKE!

This was the moment Nell had been waiting for. Out of her pocket she took the fragment of ketchup-y sheet that Dr. Livingston had brought her the night before and held it to his nose. "Fetch!" she whispered in his ear.

Dr. Livingston bounded out of his chair, trotted to the shed, and disappeared through the open doorway.

Suddenly, before the audience, a ghostly dog appeared on the scene with the ghost. The dog (looking amazingly like Dr. Livingston) grabbed the ghost's sheet with his teeth, and pulled.

"Shoo!" shrieked the ghost. "Bad dog! Let go of my sheet! You're ruining everything!"

But it was too late. Dr. Livingston pulled the ghost out of the shed, and of course, out of the scene as well. Now the dog and the "ghost" stood outside the shed, looking not so ghostly as before. In fact, they looked downright normal.

Nell and Drake ran to help Dr. Livingston.

Nell whipped the sheet off of the ghost's head. "Behold!" she cried. "The ghost of Mossy Lake!"

And there, of course, stood Frisco. "Rats. Foiled again," he said, scowling.

"Hey! No fair!" someone yelled. "I want my money back!"

"Fake!"

"Boo! Hiss!"

Drake held up his hand for silence. The crowd quieted. "What you have just witnessed is an old theater trick called 'Pepper's Ghost.' Allow my partner, Scientist Nell, to explain."

"It's quite simple really," said Nell.

"Not for me," said Frisco, frowning. "Took months of research and sneaking around after dark."

Nell unrolled a diagram she had drawn. Drake held the diagram while Nell shone a flashlight on it and explained, "To make the trick work, you must use light and glass."

"In this case," Drake hollered from behind the diagram, "a sheet of plastic that looks like glass. Works just as well."

"Indeed," agreed Nell. "When Frisco turned on the empty slide projector in the shed, it lit him up. The light was projected from him to the sheet of plastic, which is in front of all of you, except that you can't see it."

"Believe me," Drake assured them, "it's there."

"You, as the audience, saw the lighted ghost

reflected off the plastic surface, while at the same time you saw through the plastic to what lay behind it," Nell continued.

"But *reflection* isn't really the right word," commented Drake.

Shaking her head, Nell said, "No, indeed, Detective Doyle. Not the right word at all. Because reflection is what happens at the surface of the glass, while what is really happening with Pepper's Ghost occurs *behind* the glass. Imagine yourself looking into a mirror. You don't see yourself flattened on the mirror's surface, as in a photograph. Instead you see yourself in a room behind the mirror."

"Couldn't have said it better myself, Scientist Nell. While the light is reflected off the plastic glass, it *behaves* as if it were at a point in space behind the glass, creating a virtual image. That's why it looked like Sloane could walk through the ghost. The image of the ghost was behind the plastic."

"Guess I'll have to drum up some other get-rich-quick scheme," mumbled Frisco. "You guys always ruin everything."

Nell rolled up her diagram. "Show's over. Frisco will happily refund your money."

"Who said anything about happy?" complained Frisco. "Besides, it was Sloane's stupid idea."

"Was not," said Sloane.

"Was, too," said Frisco.

"Was not."

"Was, too."

Nell and Drake left them to their arguing and headed back to the car with Dr. Livingston. "Finished?" asked Mr. Doyle as they climbed in.

"Case solved," answered Nell with a satisfied sigh.

"Thanks to Nell and her hunches," added Drake. "Couldn't have done it without her."

"Ditto, Detective Doyle." And they shook hands for a job well done.

Nell buckled her seat belt and braced herself. "To my house, Mr. Doyle. And make it snappy."

"Check."

Tires squealed as they disappeared into the night.

CHAPTER EIGHT
Something Foul

It was a cloudy Wednesday afternoon, and Drake Doyle lay in bed, miserable. He had stayed home from school with a cold. A nasty cold. He sneezed. He sniffled. He blew his nose. And, every now and then, he coughed a bit as well. So you see, he was quite miserable indeed.

Just then, there was a scratch and a *sniff!* at his door. "Come in," he croaked.

And in trotted Dr. Livingston.

"Hello there," said Drake, already cheered by the visit. Dr. Livingston gave him a lick on the chops and wagged his tail hello.

After patting Dr. Livingston on the head, Drake withdrew a long, skinny roll of paper from the pouch that hung from Dr. Livingston's neck.

Written on the roll of paper was a column of letters from top to bottom. A secret code. Then, from under his bed, Drake pulled out a rolling pin. The code breaker. Taping the end of the strip of paper near one of the handles, he wound the paper around the rolling pin like a bandage. A secret message appeared, as he'd known it would.

```
DETECTIVE DOYLE —
SUSPECT SOMETHING
FOUL. MEET ME AT
NATURE HEADQUARTERS
IMMEDIATELY. I WILL
EXPLAIN EVERYTHING.
SIGNED —
NATURALIST NELL
PS — MISSED YOU TODAY
AT SCHOOL. HOPE YOU
ARE FEELING BETTER.
```

Drake forgot all about his cold. "Quick, Dr. Livingston," he cried as he pushed back the covers, "fetch my detective kit!" And even though Drake really should have stayed in bed because he had a cough and was running a slight fever, he couldn't bear to stay home knowing something foul was afoot. He was a true detective at heart.

He washed, dressed, combed his hair, and blew his nose for good measure, then quietly slipped over to Nature Headquarters with Dr. Livingston. He didn't really like slipping out without permission, but he had a job to do, nasty cold or not. He left a note on his nightstand that read:

Dear Mom,
Feeling much better. Respiration normal. Pulse regular. Call me on my cell phone if worried.
Signed,
Detective Doyle

"You look awful," said Nell, when she opened the front door.

"Thanks," he replied, trying to sound cheery even though his nose was stuffed up.

And without further ado, Nell grabbed him by his scarf, yanked him into Nature Headquarters, and shut the door.

Nature Headquarters was their secret code name for Nell's room. It made perfect sense because it looked just like a jungle. Giant papier-mâché trees loomed overhead, dangling with vines and glittery leaves. Here and there and everywhere were aquariums, terrariums, and cages filled with spiders, snakes, fish, plants, bugs, rats, and all sorts of creepy-crawlies. At any one time in her room, something was always sleeping, sneezing, snorting, scooting, scratching, scurrying, slurping, or slithering. The smells of mouse fur, fish water, and fungus filled the steamy air.

But neither steam nor smells bothered Nell Fossey. Quite simply, Nell loved nature. Nature was her specialty. Nell was a naturalist.

"What have you got?" asked Drake as he wiped the steam off his glasses.

Nell pointed to an open book on her desk. "Read that."

Drake sat and put on his glasses. "Hmm. Information on the Diamond Tipped Parrot." He began to read, jotting notes to himself in his lab notebook every once in a while. "Native to the jungles of Mexico" . . . *Ah-choo!* . . . "Almost extinct" . . . *Sniff! Honk!* . . . "Only ten Diamond Tipped Parrots left in the wild" . . . *Cough! Cough!* After Drake finished the article, he turned to Nell and said, "Fascinating indeed, but what's this got to do with us?"

"Glad you asked," said Nell, and she began to pace the room.

From the look on his partner's face, Drake knew this was serious. He braced himself for the worst.

"As you know," Nell explained, "today was Pet Day at Seaview Elementary. Everyone brought their pets and shared a little about them."

"You brought Dr. Livingston, I presume?"

"Correct. Of course there were the usual dogs and cats and rabbits, but Baloney brought something special. Quite special, I soon discovered."

Drake frowned. Usually things having to do with Baloney weren't good at all. Not only was Baloney a friend of Frisco's, but he was the hugest kid at Seaview Elementary. Now, being huge by itself wasn't a bad thing. But Baloney also loved to squish and smash and mash things, and perhaps sit on them as well. Together these became a very bad thing, especially if Baloney was sitting on your head. (Baloney's real name wasn't Baloney at all. It was Bubba Mahoney, but no one called him that. Not even his mother.)

"Baloney brought a parrot to class," Nell was saying, moving aside vines and leaves as she paced. "He said he got it from Jake McNeely's Pet Palace last weekend. Of course, when I got home I checked my mom's bird book to see what kind of parrot it was. Just curious, you know."

"Naturally."

"From the photo and description," continued Nell, "I'm almost positive that Baloney's bird is a Diamond Tipped Parrot. But that's impossible because there are only ten left in the wild. All the rest live in London as part of a breeding program. Simply put, there are no Diamond Tipped Parrots in this country."

Drake frowned again. "If it's not a Diamond Tipped Parrot"—*ah-choo!*—"then what is it?"

Nell stopped her pacing and leaned toward Drake. She lowered her voice to a whisper. "That's just it, Detective Doyle. I think it *is* a Diamond Tipped Parrot. And if it is, that means it was kidnapped from the jungles of Mexico."

Drake gasped. "Great Scott! That's against the law!"

"Precisely. It's called illegal wildlife trafficking. But it happens all the time. People kidnap exotic, endangered animals and sell them just to make a buck. It can cause the extinction of an entire species!" She paused and looked deadly serious. "That's why we must go to Jake McNeely's Pet Palace and snoop around. Immediately. Where there's one kidnapped parrot, there are bound to be more. Doyle and Fossey to the rescue!"

CHAPTER NINE
Plan A

Jake McNeely's Pet Palace was on the edge of town. The building looked like it hadn't seen a coat of paint in twenty years. Moss and ferns grew thick on the roof. A neon sign flashed hot pink: JAKE MC EEL 'S PET PALA . (A few letters were missing.) Altogether, it looked downright seedy. Just the place to buy a kidnapped parrot.

Drake came prepared. Whenever he was on assignment, he carried his detective kit. It contained all sorts of clever gizmos—periscopes, a compass, a fingerprint kit, a flashlight, a decoder, a lock pick, a glowstick, a few nifty disguises for emergency situations, and much more. (And, of course, his handy-dandy camera disguised as a teddy bear.)

Already Drake and Nell were hard at work. Hidden by a bush, they used their periscopes to peer in the window at Jake McNeely as he helped a customer buy a fish and some dog food. After the customer left, Jake counted the money in his cash register.

"Hmm," murmured Drake, "that's a pretty thick wad of money for just selling a fish and a bag of dog food. Looks like thousands of dollars." *Ah-choo!* "Maybe millions." (He would have jotted a note to himself in his lab notebook, but it was too difficult to peer through the periscope, take notes, blow his nose, and remain top secret all at the same time.)

"Not only that, but Jake's wearing alligator boots," whispered Nell, "and a belt made from a boa constrictor. For a pet-store owner, he obviously has no respect for nature."

"Agreed," said Drake. "He fits our profile precisely. But, so far, I only see one parrot, and it's not a Diamond Tipped."

"Roger that. They must be hidden somewhere." Nell put down her periscope and looked at Drake. "This calls for action. Prepare for Plan A."

"Check." *Cough!*

Five minutes later, they were ready. Nell was

dressed as a shopper, complete with lipstick, department-store bags, and a checkbook. (Fake, of course.) Drake was dressed as a tourist, with a flowered shirt, shorts, teddy-bear camera, and a very fat wallet. (Again, fake.)

"Ready, Naturalist Nell?"

"Ready, Detective Doyle."

Together they took a deep breath and entered the store.

It was dark, dingy, damp, and dirty. The air was filled with cheeps and squeaks, but they weren't happy cheeps and squeaks—they were very sad indeed. And the smell? Frankly, the place reeked.

"Can I help you?" Jake McNeely stood in front of them, looking rather mean in his alligator boots and snakeskin belt. He seemed impatient, like he didn't really want to help them at all.

For a second, Drake was at a loss for words. Fortunately, Nell was on top of things. After all, she didn't have a cold to worry about.

"Why, yes. Thank you very much," she replied, acting natural. "I'm looking for a pet, and I love insects."

Jake grunted. "Insects, is it? Well, if you want bugs, lady, we've got bugs." And he led Nell to the bug section.

Drake knew that was his cue. While Jake tried to sell Nell a praying mantis, Drake crept around, keeping his eyes peeled for parrots. So far, nothing. And then he saw it. A door. KEEP OUT! read the sign on the door. THIS MEANS YOU! Since Jake was facing the other way, Drake pushed open the door and crept in.

There were cages everywhere. Big cages. Little cages. Middle-size cages. Some of them were empty. Others held parrots. Diamond Tipped Parrots, to be exact. Nine of them.

"Aha!" Drake whispered to himself. "Just as we suspected!"

After snapping a few photos, Drake turned to leave. It was time to fetch Nell, scram, and present the evidence to the police. But before he could carry out the rest of Plan A, something terrible happened. Something awful. Something all detectives dread when they're trying to be sneaky. Drake felt a sneeze coming on. A big sneeze. A dilly of a sneeze. A whopper. He tried to hold it back. But it was no use. It was rather like holding back a volcano when it wants to erupt.

AAAAAAhhhhh-choooooooooooo!

Drake froze as the sound of his sneeze echoed throughout the store.

Suddenly all the parrots began to squawk and screech at once.

And from the other room, he heard Nell cry, "Run, Drake, run!"

But it was too late.

Jake McNeely burst into the room, dragging Nell by one arm. He grabbed Drake by his collar. They were caught. Plan A was a bust.

"Trying to mess up my scheme, are you, you little brats? I'll show you. . . ." And before Drake could smack him over the head with his teddy-bear camera, Jake shoved Nell and Drake into the biggest cage and locked it. They were trapped!

"Maybe later I'll introduce you to my pet piranhas," Jake snarled. "But for now, I'm expecting another rare delivery from Mexico." And with that, he threw back his head and laughed a sinister laugh.

As soon as the door closed behind Jake, Nell cried, "Quick, Detective Doyle, pick the lock with your handy-dandy lock picker!"

"Check!" But when Drake reached for his detective kit, it was gone. "Egads! Jake must have taken it with him!"

It was, quite possibly, the worst moment of their detective careers.

"This is awful," said Drake. *Cough! Cough!*

"Terrible," said Nell.

"We simply must do something." *Ah-choo! Honk!*

"Yes, but what?"

"What about Plan B?" asked Drake.

"There is no Plan B. There wasn't time. All we have is Plan A."

"This is awful," said Drake again. *Sniff! Sniff!*

"Terrible."

So they sat in the cage, trying not to think about being fish food. Meanwhile, Nell was getting rather hungry and Drake was wishing he had brought an extra hankie.

Then, suddenly, Drake felt something wiggling under his clothes. "Great Scott!" he screeched. "They're eating me already!" Fearing the worst, he reached inside his shirt and pulled out a . . . a . . . cell phone. The same phone that Sloane had lent him as payment for rescuing her from the laundry chute. It was set on VIBRATE.

Sick with relief, he flipped it open, wondering who could possibly be calling. "Uh—hello? I mean, Doyle and Fossey."

"Drake? Are you all right?" It was his mother.

"Uh—I don't know, Mom. I'm not feeling so good." *Ah-choo!* "I think my fever—"

Nell snatched the phone away from him. "Mrs. Doyle, this is Nell. We have an emergency. . . ." And she proceeded to give Mrs. Doyle the gory details. (You really can't blame Drake for being a little foggy in the head, because, as you well know, his nose was stuffed up and he was running a slight fever, plus he felt another sneeze coming on.)

Five minutes later, red and blue lights flashed and sirens wailed. "The jig is up," the police yelled through the megaphone. "We've got you surrounded!"

Thanks to the police, it was over in a jiffy. Jake gave himself up. Drake and Nell were released. The parrots were taken into protective custody. All in all, Plan A was a smashing success.

TV crews and reporters from the *Mossy Lake Daily Word* and *National Geographic* arrived to interview them and take their pictures. Nell gave a few speeches and held up quite well under the lights, but Drake was exhausted. He was relieved to see his parents drive up, and after them, Professor Fossey. It was time to call it a day.

"Couldn't have done it without you, Detective Doyle," said Nell, shaking his hand.

"Ditto, Naturalist Nell," said Drake.

"Get plenty of rest and call me in the morning," Nell added, patting him on the back.

"Check." *Ah-choo!*

That night, tucked in bed, with a flashlight under the covers, Drake wrote in his lab notebook:

Jake McNeely
(known as Jake the Snake)
behind bars.
A slippery fellow, according
to police.
Parrots to be returned to
jungle.
Payment: feature article in
National Geographic.
_____

Paid in full.
_____

Activities and Experiments for Super-Scientists

Contents

Your Own Lab

Serious scientists always have their own lab. It can be quite simple. A desk. A lamp. A few necessary supplies. Here are some hot tips for creating your own lab:

1. Begin collecting items you might need for experiments, such as tape, string, markers, rulers, and glass and plastic containers. You never know when they might come in handy.

2. You'll need a blank lab notebook. Like Drake and Nell, you will record every step of the experiment: procedures, observations, results, etc. And, of course, all good scientists know to record even their mistakes.

3. To be completely official, you will need a lab coat. Old shirts that button down the front work well. Using a permanent marker, write your name on the shirt. (Ask permission first.)

4. Lastly, all good scientists label everything. Keep masking tape and a marker on hand.

Good Science Tip

All scientists make mistakes. Many experiments don't turn out as expected. This is part of everyday science! If your experiments have unexpected results, try to figure out what went wrong and why. Don't be afraid to ask for help. And definitely record your mistakes in your lab notebook. Some of the greatest scientific discoveries were accidental.

Even though mistakes are a part of science, sloppiness is not. Good scientists read instructions and practice good laboratory technique.

bacteria

bacteria
mold

A Wonderful Accident

In 1928, scientist Alexander Fleming was busy conducting an experiment. He was growing bacteria in petri dishes, and the bacteria were multiplying nicely. However, when he returned after a holiday, the petri dishes had been contaminated with mold. Oops! That wasn't supposed to happen!

But he noticed something interesting. In the areas of the contaminated culture, the bacteria didn't grow. Now, Fleming could easily have thrown his experiment away and started over, but instead it got him thinking.

Why didn't the bacteria grow in the presence of the mold?

At this point, Fleming likely developed a **hypothesis**. A hypothesis is a scientist's guess as to what is happening and why. Fleming's hypothesis might have sounded something like this: *Based on my observations, I believe the mold is producing a substance that prevents the growth of bacteria.*

Fleming then set about to test his hypothesis. What he discovered changed the course of the medical world. Quite by accident, Fleming had discovered a mold called **penicillin**, which is now one of the most widely used antibiotics. Penicillin prevents the growth of bacteria. By 1940, people who might have died from infections like pneumonia could take penicillin and recover. From penicillin, the search for other antibiotics began, and now we have many to choose from.

The point is, Fleming did not set out to discover a new antibiotic. (He didn't even know what one was, since it hadn't been discovered yet!) But when things went wrong, Fleming didn't cry, panic, scream, or ignore it. Instead, like a good scientist, he wondered *why* the bacteria couldn't grow in the presence of the mold.

Blast Sloane Out of the Laundry Chute!

All right, so it's not Sloane, it's an egg. And, well, it's not a laundry chute either, it's a pipe. But TOUGH TOENAILS!!! IT'S KINDA THE SAME!!! AND BESIDES, IT'S FUN!!! (You can draw a frowny-face on the egg and pretend it's Sloane if that makes you feel better.)

MATERIALS

- PVC pipe, with a $1\frac{7}{16}$-inch inner diameter*
- sandpaper
- 1 medium hard-boiled egg**
- tablespoon
- baking soda
- tissue
- vinegar
- measuring cup
- plastic sandwich bag

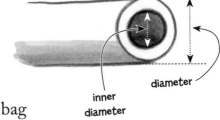

*Note #1: *Diameter* is the distance of a straight line that passes through the center of a circle.

Measure the pipe's *inner* diameter at the hardware store.

**Note #2: Large eggs are *too* large for PVC pipe. Medium eggs are just right. To hard-boil an egg, have an adult boil it in water for 15 minutes. Cool the egg before you peel it.

PROCEDURE

1. Ask a handy adult to cut the PVC pipe to a length of 7 inches. (If you buy it from a store, they will cut it for you.) Smooth any rough edges with sandpaper.

2. Peel the egg and insert it 1½ inches into the bottom of the pipe. It should be a tight fit.

3. Measure 2 tablespoons of baking soda into a tissue and fold it up tightly so that none of it leaks out. Keep it handy, because you'll need it in a hurry.

4. Pour vinegar into a measuring cup to the ¼-cup mark, then add water to the ⅓-cup mark.

5. With one hand, hold the pipe (egg side down) over a sink.

6. Put your other hand into the plastic sandwich bag. This is your glove.

7. Pour the vinegar-and-water mixture into the top of the pipe. The egg should keep the liquid from seeping through.

8. Add the entire baking-soda packet (including tissue) to the vinegar and water mixture. *Quickly* seal the top of the pipe with your gloved hand, and shake.

9. PLOP! SPLAT! Out comes the egg!

How does this work?

Vinegar and baking soda react together to form completely new substances: water, salt, and carbon-dioxide gas. So much gas is produced that it builds up pressure. The pressure forces the egg out the end of the pipe.

Soak Up Some Juice

Think about it. Capillary action might come in rather handy. You're thirsty. You're stumbling along. There's a mud puddle. You stick in your big toe and soak up some swampy water. Gulp . . . gulp . . . gulp . . . *ahh* . . .

Plants draw up water through capillary action. Tiny capillaries carry moisture and nutrients from the roots throughout the entire plant. Try this simple activity and observe capillary action "in action."

MATERIALS

- measuring spoon
- water
- clear drinking glass or jar
- red food coloring
- celery stalk with leaves

PROCEDURE

1. Measure 3–6 tablespoons of water into the jar.

2. Add enough red food coloring to turn the water blood red (about 30–40 drops).

3. Slice 1 inch off the bottom of the celery stalk, then place the stalk, cut side down, into the jar. Make sure the cut surface of the celery is completely under water.

4. Record your observations every 15 minutes for the first hour. After 3 hours, rinse off the celery and then slice it crosswise in a few different places. Where are the capillaries located? Did the dye reach the very top? Are there capillaries in the leaves?

Other Super-Scientific Stuff: Bored? Tired of twiddling your thumbs? Take a fresh white rose, trim $1/2$ inch off the end of the stem, and stick it in red-colored water (see steps #1 and #2). Leave the rose in the colored water overnight to see the full effect. And if you're feeling super creative, try putting a yellow rose in red water. What color do you think the rose will be? How about a yellow rose in blue water? A pink rose in green water? You get the idea . . .

How does this work?

Water molecules have adhesive properties—they like to stick together and to other things. (Think of a glass of ice water on a hot day. Water clings in droplets on the outside of the glass. Only when the droplets get too heavy do they fall.) In the same way, water molecules can "climb" a thin tube, such as a capillary, by clinging to the sides of the tube and to each other.

Pepper's Ghost

Picture this. London. 1863. A crowded theater. The lights dim. Suddenly everybody gasps. There, on stage, is a *ghost*. It moves and talks while other actors just walk right through it! AAAAHHHH!!!!!!

It's a hit! The audience and newspapers love it!

And so, the special effect called Pepper's Ghost was born, named after its inventor, Professor John Henry Pepper. (Before 1863, a stage ghost would likely have been an actor wearing a sheet. And if another actor had tried to walk through him, the ghost would likely have said, "Ow! You're stepping on my big toe!" or "You big clumsy knuckle-brain! Watch where you're going!" or some such.)

Scare yourself silly by making your own Pepper's Ghost.

MATERIALS

- rectangular cardboard box (at least 15 inches x 10 inches)
- ruler
- scissors
- tape
- plastic glass (Plexiglas or another brand—see step #4)
- miniature ghost model (or scary action figure)
- black cloth (such as a black T-shirt)
- small flashlight

PROCEDURE

1. Make sure that the sides of the cardboard box are taller than your ghost model or action figure.

2. Look at the diagram on page 83. Measure side B of your box with a ruler. Cut away this amount from side A. (For instance, if side B measures 12 inches, then cut away 12 inches from side A. You should have at least 3 inches remaining on side A. If you have less than 3 inches, find a different box.) Cardboard can be tough to cut. Ask an adult for help if you're having trouble.

3. With leftover cardboard from step #2, make a half wall (half the length of side B). Using tape, secure directly across from the cut end of side A. This creates a "backstage."

4. Starting from the back right corner of the half wall, measure diagonally across the stage, ending at the left front corner. This is how long your piece of plastic glass should be. It should be at least as high as the cardboard box. Secure the plastic glass with tape. (Plastic glass—sometimes called Plexiglas—is available from hardware stores and some craft supply stores. They will cut the plastic glass for you. *Do not* attempt to cut it yourself. Edges may be sharp, so be careful!)

5. Place the ghost in the backstage opening. (It works best if you place a black cloth under and around the ghost so that the sides of the cardboard box aren't reflected.)

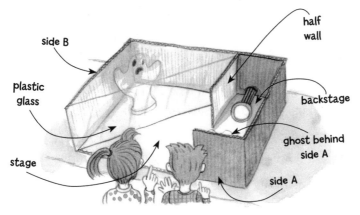

6. Prop up a flashlight "backstage" so that it will shine directly on the ghost model.

7. Turn on flashlight.

8. Flip off room lights.

9. Scream.

Disclaimer: Not responsible for broken windows in your mad dash to escape. Not responsible for eyeballs popping out from fright. Good cure for hiccups.

How does this work?

Light from the flashlight shines onto the ghost model, lighting it up. The light is then projected from the ghost and reflects off the plastic glass back to you, the viewer. But *reflection* really isn't the right word, because reflection is what happens at the surface of the glass, while what is really happening with Pepper's Ghost occurs *behind* the glass. While the light is reflected off the glass surface, it *behaves* as if it were at a point in space behind the glass, creating a *virtual image* of the lighted object.

Again, a mirror is a good example. You don't view your reflection as being flat on the mirror's surface, as in a poster. Instead, you see yourself in a room behind the mirror. Of course, all of this is an *illusion*. There is no one behind the mirror, any more than there is a ghost behind the glass. What would Sloane have seen as she walked bravely through the ghost image? Nothing.

Send a Secret Message

How did Nell write the secret message in Chapter Eight urging Drake to hurry over to Nature Headquarters? Writing and decoding the same secret message is easy—once you know how. Follow these simple steps for some super-sleuthing techniques of the secret sort.

MATERIALS

- scissors
- paper
- clear tape
- rolling pin or paper-towel tube
- pen

PROCEDURE

1. Cut strips of paper ½-inch wide.

2. Tape the strips of paper end to end, until you have one very loooonnnng piece of paper.

3. Tape one end of the strip to one end of the rolling pin. Draw a dot on the end of the paper strip to indicate where the message begins.

4. Wrap the paper around the rolling pin as if you were wrapping a mummy. The edges should touch each other, but not overlap. Tape other end in place. (Cut the paper strip if it is too long.)

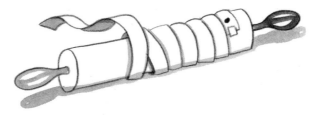

5. Using one paper segment for each letter, write your message.

6. Send your roll of paper to your partner. (Never fear. If it is intercepted, it will look like nonsense.)

7. To read, your partner simply wraps your message around a rolling pin or cylinder of the *exact* same diameter, beginning with the dot.

(Paper-towel tubes, tin cans, and soda cans are some examples of cylinders that would work.)

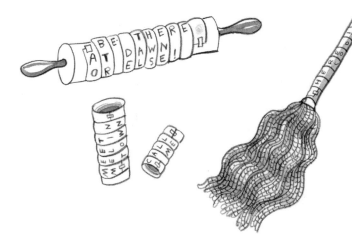

Good Science Tip

If you use a paper-towel tube to create your message, your friend will not be able to decode it with a tin can. The diameter is the key to getting the letters in the message to line up just right. Make sure that you and your fellow detectives have cylinders with identical diameters, or else your secret messages will be more like secret *messes!*

Serious Business

In Chapter Nine, "Plan A," Drake disguised himself as a tourist, while Nell dressed up as a shopper. Ready for undercover operations. Ready to nab Jake the Snake.

The illegal wildlife trade is serious business. Criminals like Jake the Snake get rich, while animal populations disappear from wild habitats. Some even become extinct. The sad fact is that the U.S. and Europe are the *leading* consumers of illegal wildlife products, whether it's a live parrot or a carving made from elephant ivory.

While you won't be doing any investigation into the illegal wildlife trade, you can certainly do your part by becoming a smart shopper and a top-notch tourist. Here are some tips:

1. If your family decides to purchase an unusual pet, such as a parrot or exotic reptile, be certain it is captive bred. Many animals that are illegal if caught in the wild are perfectly legal when born and raised in captivity by a

licensed breeder. Before a parrot chick is three weeks old, the breeder slips a seamless, coded, metal band onto the chick's leg. The chick is now *closed-banded*. This ensures that the bird was not captured in the wild.

Be a smart shopper and know what you're getting into. Check out the following Web sites for more information:

- www.birdsnways.com/wisdom/ww7e.htm
- www.birdsnways.com/articles/efjul3.htm
- http://animal.discovery.com/guides/reptiles/reptiles.html

2. If you're feeling under the weather and need some medicine, be aware that many medicines from Asia contain such things as tiger bones and rhinoceros horn. Know the ingredients! Be a smart shopper and don't buy these products!

3. If you're traveling as a tourist, it's a good idea to stay away from *any* product—ivory, tortoiseshell, fur, feathers, skins, etc.—made from animals. By

buying these items, you are often unknowingly supporting illegal hunting (also called *poaching*).

4. When traveling, don't allow your photo to be taken next to a baby animal such as a baby chimpanzee or a tiger cub. What tourists don't realize is that often the animal mother was killed just to kidnap the baby. Charging money for photographs is a way for these kidnappers (called *poachers*) to make a living. While this example doesn't necessarily cross international borders, tourism makes it possible. Be a top-notch tourist and don't say cheese!

Did you know?
Recently a smuggler like Jake the Snake was arrested while attempting to leave his country with illegal wildlife. What was the wildlife? you ask. Lizards. A dozen of them. And where did he hide the lizards? you ask. In his underwear! Yikes!

How Can You Help?

Many animal populations are endangered because of habitat destruction. You can help reclaim vital habitats by clicking onto a few Web sites each day. It's free, simple, and fun.

www.ecologyfund.com—The Ecology Fund helps parrots by purchasing parrot habitats in Mexico.

www.redjellyfish.com—Red Jellyfish purchases sections of the rainforest and also feeds orphaned chimps.

http://rainforest.care2.com—In addition to purchasing rainforest, Care2 purchases bamboo forests for pandas, and habitats for big cats such as tigers, jaguars, and snow leopards.

www.thehungersite.com—Not only does the hunger site provide food for the hungry, but it helps protect habitats such as rainforests.